THE
FALL GUY

THE
FALL GUY

BARBARA FRADKIN

RAVEN BOOKS
an imprint of
ORCA BOOK PUBLISHERS

Library and Archives Canada Cataloguing in Publication

Fradkin, Barbara Fraser, 1947-
The fall guy / Barbara Fradkin.
(Rapid reads)

Issued also in electronic formats.
ISBN 978-1-55469-835-6

I. Title. II. Series: Rapid reads
PS8561.R233F34 2011   C813'.6   C2010-908113-7

First published in the United States, 2011
Library of Congress Control Number: 2010942252

Summary: Handyman Cedric O'Toole is set up to take the fall for a murder he didn't commit. He'll need all his inventive power to save himself. (RL 4.0)

Orca Book Publishers is dedicated to preserving the environment and has printed this book on paper certified by the Forest Stewardship Council.

Orca Book Publishers gratefully acknowledges the support for its publishing programs provided by the following agencies: the Government of Canada through the Canada Book Fund and the Canada Council for the Arts, and the Province of British Columbia through the BC Arts Council and the Book Publishing Tax Credit.

Design by Teresa Bubela
Cover photography by Getty Images

ORCA BOOK PUBLISHERS
PO Box 5626, Stn. B
Victoria, BC Canada
V8R 6S4

ORCA BOOK PUBLISHERS
PO Box 468
Custer, WA USA
98240-0468

www.orcabook.com
Printed and bound in Canada.

14 13 12 11 • 4 3 2 1

To Leslie, Dana and Jeremy

CHAPTER ONE

The first hint of trouble was when I saw the big black Buick roaring down my lane. I didn't recognize the car. But the way the guy drove, he was either showing off or too stupid to realize he'd blow his shocks in six months. Too late, he slammed on the brakes and skidded to a stop in a spray of gravel, flattening my front gate. It was an old gate, hanging by a piece of chicken wire, but still...

A few choice swear words came to my mind but died when the guy unfolded himself from the car. Six foot and easily two-fifty. Beer gut and a couple of extra chins, but I doubted that would slow him down much.

He wiped the dust off his bumper and inspected it. That seemed to take forever, as if he was daring me to start something. I didn't, even though I could feel my blood beginning to boil.

Finally he shrugged, reached into his front seat and took out an envelope.

"Are you Cedric Elvis O'Toole?"

I should have just said yes, but I didn't like his tone. Besides, I hadn't been called that in so long I'd almost forgotten it was my real name. What can I say? My mother had always expected Elvis to sweep in and marry her, but he died the day I was born. When she got over her shock, she decided Cedric would make a better name for a doctor anyway.

When you're from a scrubby backcountry farm, who was going to set you straight?

I've been calling myself Rick ever since Barry Mitchell laughed out loud at roll call the first day of kindergarten.

"Who's asking?" I said instead.

"Jonathan Miller from Hopper, James and Elliston, Attorneys at Law."

That was my second hint of trouble. There's only one law firm in the township, and Hopper and his pals aren't it. But before I could even reply, he slapped the fat brown envelope in my hand.

"Consider yourself served."

"With what?"

"A summons to appear in court."

I let the envelope fall to the ground. A million thoughts raced through my head. Had the tax guys finally caught me? I'm just a simple handyman trying to give myself and my customers a break on the occasional job.

Not the big ones that require permits or guarantees, just the little fix-its like painting the shed or repairing the chain saw. I need that couple of bucks way more than the tax man does.

"What for?"

Mr. Fancy Car smirked. The guy had no class. Take away the blue suit and the skinny tie, and he was just a goon. "My job is to deliver it, not read it."

He was standing there, hands in his pockets, like he was waiting for some answer. I bent down and dusted the thing off. It felt thick enough to hold down a tarp in a gale. I started to sweat. Legal documents—in fact, just about any document—made me sweat. But I tried to look cool as I tore open the flap and pulled out a stack of papers. They looked very official, like the ones I got for this piece of scrub when my mother died. She called it a farm, but no one had been able to grow anything on it except weeds for years.

I could see the guy looking around, taking in the scrap heap of rusted cars and engine bits all over the yard. I liked to invent things. Who knew when a broken lawn mower might come in handy? There were more bits of engine and metal inside the sheds. When I ran out of room for my inventions, I built another shed. The result wasn't pretty, but it had been a few years since I'd tried to impress anybody.

I did keep a few chickens and a goat, but they didn't exactly improve the look of the place. And out back on the sunny side of the barn, there was a vegetable patch I was pretty proud of. When you're an inventor still looking for that big break, you don't have a lot of spare cash to throw around in supermarkets.

Thinking about money brought me back to the papers in my hand. Even without reading them, I knew this was going to cost me money. I scanned the front page and made out the words *plaintiff* and *defendant*. Then the name in bold letters right in the middle stopped me cold.

Jeffrey Wilkins

2 Wilkins Point Road

I'd just done a job for Jeff Wilkins. A big job, building a new deck on his fancy waterfront cottage. We'd squeezed it in just under the size limit. So no permit, no paperwork, no taxes. My mouth went dry.

I put on some bluster. "What is all this about? Somebody complained?"

The smirk grew wider. "Don't you read the papers? Watch the news?"

"No," I snapped. I never read the paper. My jerry-rigged TV antenna did a fine job of getting me the hockey games and nature shows I liked to watch, but I never bothered with the news. Who wanted to know what big-city drug dealers and snake-oil politicians were up to anyway?

Then he said the words I was most afraid of hearing.

"You might want to get yourself a good lawyer."

CHAPTER TWO

As soon as Mr. Fancy Car peeled out of there, I was on the phone to Aunt Penny. I didn't have much money, but I did splurge on a phone. When you lived five miles down a gravel road, how else were customers going to contact you for that big job? Aunt Penny owned the little grocery store on the main highway that runs through the village of Lake Madrid. If you don't count the cottagers, Lake Madrid has maybe six hundred people, none of them from Spain. Someone was dreaming big.

Penny's Grocery has been there for at least a hundred years, and the floors tell the tale. The cottage people never shopped there—they used the big supermarket farther away—but the locals knew it's where all the gossip was. Aunt Penny stocked milk from Gerry's farm and corn from Ripple's down the road, instead of all that stuff trucked in from Peru. Everyone stopped in to pick up gossip along with their lottery ticket and their DVD for the night.

That day, Aunt Penny sounded run off her feet.

"I got some legal documents here about the Wilkins job," I said. "Do you know what that's about?"

"I can hardly tell that, can I, Rick, with you there and me here?"

"But I mean, has there been anything in the news?"

"About Wilkins? Oh, you mean his wife." She stopped and I could hear her talking to a customer. I thought about Wilkins' wife. I'd seen quite a lot of her when I was working. A tiny blond who flitted around inside the house like a trapped chickadee. Wilkins hadn't given her a car, so she was stuck at the cottage watching *American Idol* and decorating shows all day. She was so bored she even tried talking to me.

Aunt Penny was back on the line. "Look, Rick, I got a lineup here. You better bring the papers over and I'll have a look."

I hated running to Aunt Penny with my troubles. You never knew when she was going to bite your head off. Nothing warm and fuzzy about Aunt Pen. But she always seemed to sort things out. I loved the insides of an engine, and I was good with my hands, but not so much with people. I didn't actually stutter anymore, but, boy, sometimes I got so tied up in knots I just wanted to bolt from the room.

There were a whole lot of people at Aunt Penny's when I walked in. I knew every single one of them, but that didn't make it any easier. I've been the butt of jokes among the locals ever since my lawn-mower-powered scarecrow blew up and scared the Canada geese from Ripple's cornfield clear into the next county, along with most of his corn.

"Hey, Rick," said Bert Landry, piling his groceries on the counter. "That old tractor of mine mowed its last blade of grass yesterday. You interested?"

One time a few years back, I had fourteen tractor lawn mowers in my back field before I put my foot down. Now I'd learned to laugh and shake my head. "I hear they make good scarecrows," I said. A line Aunt Penny had taught me.

Laughter and more teasing, as the crowd worked its way through the cash. Finally I was face-to-face with Aunt Penny. All five feet, steel-gray eyes of her.

"What have you done this time, Ricky?"

"I got a summons from a law firm," I said. "Something to do with the job I did for Jeff Wilkins."

She took the papers and figured out the legal mumbo jumbo for me in a flash. That's why I go to her, even though she gives me grief.

"Jeff Wilkins is suing you for the shoddy job you did on his deck," she said.

I was outraged. I may cut corners with the tax guy, but only to give the customer and me a break. My work is never shoddy. If there's one thing I know, it's how to put things together so they work. Every inch of that fancy western-red-cedar deck had been perfect. Every screw, every cantilever, every support beam and rail.

"Can he do that? Just 'cause he feels like it?"

"He can do anything he likes, Ricky. He's got lots of money for lawyers. Has he paid you for the job?"

I pretended to think about it, but I knew the answer. Wilkins had said he was expecting a big payment next week from a bakery that bought a new fleet of trucks, but right now he had a small cash flow problem. An unlikely story. Everybody knew Wilkins was the richest man in the county, but tight as a drum when it came to parting with his money.

Aunt Penny read the answer in my red face. "Jumpin' Jiminy, Rick. When are you going to learn?"

I wasn't great with words, but this didn't make sense. "If he's got the money for fancy lawyers, how come he had no money to pay me? I bet those guys charge ten times more an hour!"

Aunt Penny was silent. That's unusual for her. She didn't look at me, also unusual. A customer came in and bought some milk, some fireworks and a lottery ticket. Aunt Penny never even exchanged the time of day. I started to get a sick feeling in my stomach.

"What's going on, Aunt Penny?" I asked once the customer left.

"Well, the thing is, Ricky, there was a problem with that deck. Yesterday afternoon, Jeff Wilkins' wife was out on it, and she leaned over the rail to reach something, and the rail gave way."

A jolt of panic shot through me. Impossible! "What! She must have been...," I sputtered, looking for an explanation. Maybe she climbed up on it, or... "Was she drunk?"

"I don't know if she was drunk, Ricky. But I don't think the courts will care. She's dead."

CHAPTER THREE

I spotted the black and white suv just after I swung into my lane. There was no turning back. The plume of dust behind me gave me away even if I'd had any place else to go. I slowed the truck so I could take stock and figure out what to say.

As far as I could see, there was just one cop. He looked small standing on the front stoop, his hat pulled low and his hands on his hips. He was looking out over my yard, watching the goat nibbling the daisies by the chicken coop. Chevie, my collie mix, was sitting at his feet, wagging her tail. Some watchdog.

I pulled the old truck to a stop and was about to get out when the cop turned toward me. I froze. It was a woman, hardly older than me. Even with the vest, the gun belt and the huge wraparound sunglasses, there was no hiding those curves. Or the long blond ponytail hanging down her back. I thought I knew all the cops at the local detachment, but this was a new one.

She stepped off the porch. "Cedric O'Toole?"

Heat rushed up my neck. I knew I was bright red, and that didn't help me find my tongue. I just nodded.

"You live here?" she asked. Heavy on the *live*.

I looked around my yard. Weeds had grown up through the rusted-out Ford on blocks by the door. They were covered in bright purple flowers, but still...There were more weeds around the tractors and washing machines down by the barn. The goat wasn't doing her job. I guess daisies are tastier than thistles.

I didn't think the cop expected an answer, so again I just nodded.

She stepped another two feet closer, her sunglasses hiding her eyes. But her mouth curved, like she was secretly laughing at me. "You make a living out here?"

"It suits me," I mumbled. "I do repairs and stuff."

"They warned me about you down at the station. Live in your own dream world, but you're no trouble. I hope they're right." She pulled out a notebook and pencil. "I'm Constable Swan, and I need to ask you a few questions."

The afternoon sun was beating down. Constable Swan didn't seem to notice, but sweat soaked my shirt. "What about?"

"Two weeks ago you completed a deck at Jeffrey Wilkins' cottage, is that correct?"

No point in denying that. The whole county knew. Rumor was Wilkins had been too cheap to hire a real contractor, that's why I got the job. Half the price and no taxes.

"Can I see the plans and the permit for that job?"

"Is there some problem?"

"Would you get the plans, please? County office doesn't have them."

"I-I...It might take awhile to find them. Is there a rush?"

She frowned and wrote in her notebook. In the silence I felt the sun burning. Finally she took off her sunglasses and looked up at me. She had amazing blue eyes. No makeup, but she didn't need it. The sun burned hotter.

"Mr. O'Toole, this is a very serious matter. An individual has died, and there have been questions raised about the quality of your deck. Mr. Wilkins is alleging that you cut corners in order to cut costs."

"That's bullshit. That deck is solid as a tank. Mr. Wilkins was the one who wanted to cut costs, not me."

"But you're not the one who's friends with the police chief. Wilkins is talking about criminal negligence, even manslaughter. These are very serious charges, Mr. O'Toole. So if you have proof that the deck is solid and the cost-cutting ideas were Wilkins', not yours, then you'd better produce them."

I looked at the ground. Criminal negligence. Manslaughter. Holy Crap. I'd had to argue with Wilkins every step of the way. About the thickness of boards, the spacing of joists, even the height of the railing. But if it came down to my word against his, I was a dead man.

I felt my face flush as fear raced up my body. "There are no plans. Not on paper. Just in my head."

Her head shot up. Her blue eyes narrowed. "No plans? No permit?"

"It didn't need a permit. Not... technically."

"No inspection? No one else checking over the plans?"

I shook my head miserably. "I know what I'm doing. I know code, and the design was solid."

"Then why did the railing give way the first time someone leaned on it, Mr. O'Toole?"

"I don't know." I didn't understand how that could happen, but I didn't feel up to explaining screws and spindles. Constable Swan continued to glare. "It shouldn't have," I added lamely. "I've done lots of decks."

"Then provide us with something in writing. Draw up the design and the specs you followed."

I was starting to feel mad. It felt better than fear. "What does Mr. Wilkins say I did wrong?"

She was already heading to her suv. She barely paused. "Just get the specs."

I yanked open the door to my own truck. "Then I'll just go over there and ask him."

She spun around. "Mr. O'Toole, you are not—I repeat, not—to contact Jeffrey Wilkins for any reason. Is that clear?"

I said nothing. Sometimes that's a good thing. She glared at me a minute longer before climbing into her suv. She rolled down the window. "And until our investigation is complete, don't leave the county either."

Then she was off in a swirl of dust.

CHAPTER FOUR

I didn't even take time to wipe the dust from my eyes. I just grabbed my tool kit, camera and keys and headed for my truck. Chevie was one step ahead of me, but I sent her back to sit on the porch. For some reason she finds riding around with me much more fun than trying to keep the chickens in the coop or the crows off the vegetable patch. Which is what I'd really like her to do.

I was so upset I forgot to baby my old truck as we hammered down the lane and along the dirt road to the highway. I hung on to the steering wheel for my life as potholes sent us both flying. I covered the ten miles to Jeff Wilkins' cottage in less than ten minutes. All the way, I worried about what I would say. Wilkins was a powerful man. Everybody bought their trucks from him. He could see that I never got another job in the county as long as he lived. If he was lying to cover his own butt, I didn't know how I was going to prove it. I didn't have too many friends in the county who would take my side over his. Worse, no other contractors were going to back up my design after I'd been undercutting them for years. I was small fry, and I liked it that way, but business was tight for everybody.

I reached the Wilkins' place before I'd thought up a plan. My nerves started to act up at the sight of the place. It was all alone on the clifftop, looking down on the lake below. More like a fort than a cottage. Huge square timber logs the color of wild honey, a red steel roof that gleamed in the sun.

A triple garage where he kept his precious cars. Wilkins was tight but only when it came to others. Mrs. Wilkins had no car and had to beg every time she wanted to borrow one, but Jeff always got the latest-model toys for himself. A sports coupe, a heavy-duty truck and a high-end suv. Traded in every year.

Lucky for me, there was no sign of any of those vehicles when I arrived. I crunched over the empty gravel parking lot and parked my truck up against the side of the house. I let out a breath I didn't know I was holding. Now I had a plan. There would be no accusations, no arguments and denials. No tongue tied in knots by a man six inches taller than me and a million dollars richer.

Just me, my camera and tape, and the deck where the poor woman fell to her death. I felt sick as that thought finally hit my reluctant brain. My fault or not, that poor, lonely woman was dead.

I walked around to the front of the house overlooking the lake. The deck was beautiful. The smell of fresh cedar still hung in the air, but the space was filled with flower boxes, patio furniture, and a big red umbrella.

Plus a gaping hole in the railing over the steepest drop.

Yellow police tape was tied across the hole. It was too flimsy to save anyone, but I wasn't worried as I walked across the deck. I'm not afraid of heights. I remembered the spot where the hole now was. It had been a terrible place to work. The house sat on a big slab of granite, and at this point the granite fell away in a sharp drop. I had to cantilever the edge of the deck out over the cliff and I'd reinforced it six ways to Sunday to be sure it was safe.

Truth was, I'd wanted to put the deck farther over, on safer ground. But Wilkins held firm. The view of the lake was breathtaking from here, he said. You feel like you're floating on air, up in the canopy of the trees growing down below.

I stood at the edge of the deck and peered over. The drop was at least twenty feet. Below, nothing but bare rock and more police tape waving in the wind. I walked back across the deck and circled around and down the rocks till I was right below the broken spot. A couple of splinters of wood were all that was left of the railing. It looked like someone had tried to clean up all trace of the accident. But looking closely, I could see gouges and scrapes in the lichen-covered granite and smears of dark red that someone had tried to wash up. The ants were having a field day. I shuddered.

I forced myself not to think about her. Instead, I looked up. An old white pine grew as tall and straight as a ship's mast from the base of the cliff. Its jagged boughs spread high above the deck. Some bark had been torn from its thick trunk halfway down, where she'd tried to grab hold. Looking farther up, I saw something I'd missed before. A bird feeder, the fancy kind meant to keep squirrels away, was attached to the trunk just above the deck. It was crooked. It was hard to tell from where I was, but it seemed to be hanging from one screw, only half screwed in. Like someone hadn't finished the job.

I started to pick my way back across the rocks to the stone steps so I could get a better look. The rumble of an engine stopped me in my tracks. It was deep and rough, like a lion purring. It had faulty timing and a hole just starting in its muffler. A big engine, but not a truck. An old Ford V8 if I was right. I tried to think who drove a car like that but drew a blank.

It crunched across the gravel and came to a stop. I ducked behind some bushes out of sight. I knew that was pretty pointless since my truck was sitting there in plain view in the parking lot. But I wanted to know what I was up against. I wanted to see the driver before he saw me. So I listened.

The engine knocked a few times before it died. Silence closed in. Even the birds seemed to be waiting. A car door slammed with a heavy clunk, and I heard footsteps on the gravel. Slow and uneven, as if the guy was marking time. I held my breath as the footsteps came near. I'm not a big guy, hitting five-ten if I stand on my toes, but I wished I'd picked a bigger bush to hide behind. The sun was low in the sky, glaring off the lake and turning everything to bright gold. The footsteps stopped, and I could imagine the guy eyeing my truck. I peeked over the bush, but couldn't see around the house.

Then the car door opened again. Springs squawked as he got back in. The engine roared to life, revved by a heavy, impatient foot on the gas. I listened as the tires spun, spraying gravel against the metal of my truck. The car rocketed down the lane, sliding on the curves and thudding over the bumps, once even bottoming out on the big rock in the middle of the road. The guy must have been going over forty miles an hour. On that rocky, one-lane track, he was either nuts or in a serious rush.

I let out my breath. I stood up slowly, unfolding my stiff muscles. Who the hell was that, and what was he up to? After three weeks on the job, I knew Wilkins' three vehicles by sound as well as by sight. None of them had that rich, muscle-car growl.

Some people are ghouls. They like to see blood and gore. They want to set eyes on the place where death had been. I thought it was disgusting, but there's no accounting for taste. When my mother piled into that rock face on the highway up past the village, people came from all over just to shake their heads. And to wonder how come she didn't see it staring right at her. How come she missed that easy turn. I never went there. Not after the first time the police took me to ID what was left of the car. I knew my mother hadn't seen the rock. Or the turn. It was January and the scrub farm was under three feet of snow. She'd have been off in a daydream, picturing herself on a tropical beach somewhere with a mai tai in her hand and a rich guy massaging her feet.

I stood looking down at the ants crawling over the bloodstained rock. That's probably what it was. Some rubbernecker come to see where Mrs. Wilkins' head cracked open on the rocks. Maybe they thought no one was home, until they spotted my truck. I thought about going up to the parking lot to check out the damage to my truck, but decided not to.

A few more dings weren't going to make any difference, and the sun was almost set. The last fingers of sunlight barely reached the rock. Soon I wouldn't be able to see, and the mosquitoes would arrive for their evening feast.

I tried to picture what had happened. What Mrs. Wilkins had been doing on the deck. Most days I was working, she'd stayed inside. It was hot out, and my sander and table saw were always running. They aren't the newest, so there was lots of sawdust and noise. Sometimes I saw her through the glass, pouring herself a drink. Nothing heavy, just wine. As often as not she'd give me a little wave. I never saw her falling down drunk, but maybe that day she had more than most. Or maybe she didn't care enough to be careful. I got the feeling she didn't care about much.

Most of the railing bits had been cleared away from the rocks, like someone was trying to get rid of the reminder. I picked up a short piece of two-by-two. Part of a spindle. One end was splintered, but the other was tapered where it would have been attached to the bottom rail. There was a hole for the screw, but it looked wrong. Too wide. I use decking screws. They're three inches long and thin so they won't split the wood as I drill them in. I've looked at a thousand holes made by decking screws. They were smaller and finer than this one.

I set the piece of wood down on the rock, puzzled. Maybe the screw had worked itself loose. Maybe Mrs. Wilkins had leaned over the edge to look at the view. In her excitement she tugged at the rail until the screw widened the hole. I shook my head in disbelief. It didn't make sense! The spindles were three inches apart. Even if one worked loose, fifteen others would hold.

The last of the setting sun was shining on the granite, lighting up its black and pink streaks. Deep in the crack between two rocks, I saw a flash of silver. I reached in and pulled out the piece of metal. Not silver at all, but steel. A stubby screw that still had bits of cedar stuck to its threads. The decking screws I used were brass, rust-resistant and three inches long. This one was a cheap alloy, half an inch too short and way too thick.

Someone had changed the screws on my railing.

CHAPTER FIVE

As I stood there staring at the screw, my brain refused to understand. Why would someone change the screws? To get me in trouble? To get out of paying me the miserable few thousand I was owed? I thought about Wilkins' lawsuit, slapped on me before the blood was even dry in his wife's death. That guy had sure been fast off the mark.

I should tell the police. I knew the screw was evidence, proof that I hadn't been negligent and that someone else had caused the accident. Then I remembered Constable

Swan's expression as she'd looked around my farm. She thought I was an idiot. Or at best, a wing nut. She'd ordered me to stay away from Wilkins' place. She might think I'd planted the screw. I should put it back where I found it and tell the police to take another look around.

Tires growled on the gravel up above. I shoved the screw in my pocket and was heading for my bush again when I heard a car door slam.

"O'Toole?" A raw roar.

Wilkins. He steamed around the edge of the house like a bull on a charge, all six feet four inches and three hundred pounds of him. Most of that fat, but still…At one-fifty after a full platter of wings, I wouldn't stand a chance. I hustled back up onto the deck and tried to look harmless. He skidded to a stop six inches from my face. The past couple of days hadn't been good ones for him. His face was puffy and purple, like he'd gone ten rounds with Mike Tyson. His eyes were bloodshot, and a blast of booze breath rolled over me.

"What the fuck do you think you're doing!"

"S-sorry about your wife, Mr. Wilkins," I started. "I just came to see—"

"See what? See how she died? With her head cracked open on those rocks is how!" Spittle flew. "Your goddamn useless railing came off right in her hands when she leaned on it!"

"I don't understand how—"

"You're going down, O'Toole! The cops showed me the screws. Cheap, half screwed in, some missing altogether. Folks warned me about you. About how your head's in the clouds and you're always dreaming up cockamamy schemes to fix things that never work. Everything you touch turns to shit, O'Toole! I should never have hired you."

I could feel the red starting up my neck. He was hulking over me. I had to force myself not to back up. I stared up at him. "I didn't use cheap screws, Mr. Wilkins. You saw how careful I was. You even said you were glad I was taking my time to get it right. Instead of trying to rush the job like other guys might." It was a long speech for me, but I was mad, and I always talk better when I'm mad.

"If you did such a great job, why did the railing crack like kindling the first time she leaned on it, you moron?" He stormed across the deck and waved out over the cliff. "She was just hanging this bird feeder, for Pete's sake. For me!" He stopped. Snorted like a bull trying to catch his breath. He was shaking all over. "I bought it for her birthday. I don't even care about goddamn birds, and she died for them!"

He was doing a good imitation of a guy who cared about his wife. I even thought

I saw a tear shining in his eyes, but they were pretty bloodshot anyway. He'd hardly paid any attention to her while she was alive. But now suddenly he was all broken up. I remembered the cheap screw in my pocket. Someone had done that deliberately.

I started to get an uneasy feeling. "Did you know she was going to hang it on that tree?"

"Yeah. She said this way we could watch the birds from the deck and from the dining-room window."

I walked over to join him. He seemed calmer now, less likely to pick me up and throw me over the edge. I looked up at the feeder and out over the cliff, trying to picture how it played out. Mrs. Wilkins was really short, and she would have had to stretch to reach the tree. Juggling the feeder, the screwdriver and the screw would have been tricky. No hand left over to hang on with.

Add to that the bottle of wine she usually put away over the afternoon…

"Was it getting dark?" I asked. By evening, she was well into the second bottle.

"I should get rid of the damn thing. She was waiting for me to hang it, and she got fed up. I kept meaning to, but work's been busy. I didn't expect her…" He snorted again and swung on me. "Who expects this? I meant to hang it! She should have known that. I'm a busy man, but goddamn it, I would have done it! But she never was any good at waiting. Always wanting things right now."

I thought about Mrs. Wilkins wandering around the TV room hour after hour, doing her nails and playing solitaire. Only the wine bottle and her phone to keep her company while she waited for him to come home. Often late in the evening, when I was packing up my tools, there was still no sign of him. And if he did come home, all he wanted was supper. Which, more often than not, she forgot to cook.

I didn't say anything. I was still trying to find out what happened. Those screws hadn't changed themselves, but I didn't want to come right out and accuse him. "Did you show the deck to anyone? Before it broke, I mean. Did anyone say anything about the screws or the railing?"

He peered at me through narrowed eyes. "Nobody looked at the outside, if that's what you mean. She was planning a party this weekend to show it off, that's why she wanted the bird feeder up. But nobody had seen the finished product yet. You can't weasel out of this one, O'Toole."

"Maybe she showed someone? While you were at work, I mean?"

"She always complained nobody would come out here. I don't even think she had any friends anymore. But what the hell does that matter? You made the deck. She fell to her death!"

He turned away from the railing and headed across the deck toward the cottage. Night had fallen, and the sensor lights from the security system blinded us. For a second he looked like a monster, his face a mask of rage in the yellow light.

"Get the hell out of here, O'Toole," he snarled. "I know what you're trying to do. Weasel out and see if you can pin the blame on someone else for your own screwup. If I see you here again, Lori-Anne might not be the only one with her head cracked open on the rocks!"

I scurried away. Gunning my truck down his gravel drive, I couldn't help thinking he'd taken the thought straight out of my head.

Only it was him who was responsible, and him trying to pin the blame on someone else. Me. But I didn't think it was a screwup. I think it had worked out just the way he wanted.

CHAPTER SIX

Halfway home, I started to shake. That's when it hit me what a big mess I was in. I had no design plans. No final inspection reports. No proof I used the right screws and someone else had replaced them. The only man who could vouch for my construction specs was at the top of my suspect list. First off, that grieving-widower act stank more than three-day-old fish. He'd treated the woman like something on a junk heap. Now suddenly he's all broken up about her death. He knew she was the impatient type, but he'd stalled for days about hanging her new bird feeder. Had he guessed she'd get fed up and try it herself? Did he know it would be nearly impossible without using two hands and leaning hard on the rail?

Does a guy need a reason to bump off his wife? Since I'd never had a real girlfriend, I couldn't guess. I remember wanting to kill Mary Ellen Potts when she dumped me after only two weeks. She'd been the one asking me out in the first place. Until she found out Mom's farm wasn't worth a penny. Some women would do just about anything to move up in the world, Aunt Penny explained. Which hardly made me feel better.

I didn't know much about Lori-Anne Wilkins, but maybe she was the same. Aunt Penny said she flamed early and burned out quick. She grew up somewhere down east but had followed a sweet-talker who told her about the good life in the city. They never made it past the trailer park on the west side of town.

After ten years he took off, leaving her with two kids, a pile of maxed-out credit cards and a junk-heap car that didn't run when the temperature went below freezing. She earned money cleaning houses and tending bar till Jeff Wilkins turned up. He must have seemed like the answer to her dreams.

Some dream.

The road was pitch-black and the only light was from farms along the way. There was only one other car, shining its high beams far in the distance behind me. I peered at Aunt Penny's store as I passed by, hoping the light was still on. The store was dark, but her windows were lit up on the second floor where she lived. I pulled into the gravel parking lot.

"Twice in one day, Ricky," she said as I climbed the stairs.

I knew I was going to owe her, but I was wound up too tight to care.

"I think Jeff Wilkins is trying to set me up," I said.

She didn't roll her eyes. She didn't snort or reach over to feel my forehead. She poured me a glass of whisky and looked me in the eye.

"Why?"

"Someone changed the screws on that railing. I think it was him. I think he was trying to kill his wife."

"Why?"

"I don't know, maybe he was tired of her or something."

She got up, poured herself a shot and lit a cigarette. Then she stood looking at me. "Why you?"

I didn't have a clear answer to that. Usually Aunt Penny didn't make me do all the thinking.

"Maybe he thinks I'm too dumb to fight back?"

She blew out a stream of smoke. Looked at me some more. "Were you messing round with Lori-Anne, Ricky?"

My jaw dropped. It made it hard to talk even if I could have found words. I'd felt sorry for her, but messing around didn't come that easy to me.

Aunt Penny shook her head impatiently. "Jeff Wilkins is a jealous man. Did you spend time with her? Talk to her?"

"Well, I talked to her, yeah. I mean, she was there. She said things to me and I answered. Just to be friendly!" I thought about it. "She made me lunch a couple of times. She had nothing to do all day, and she had no car, so she…"

"She came on to you," Aunt Penny said. She looked disgusted.

"Well, no. She…" I stopped. A penny dropped. Wilkins had come upon us once, having lunch. Lori-Anne had brought me a beer because it was hot. She was laughing. It was a nice change and it made me smile. Wilkins had picked up my beer, poured it on the ground, crushed the can and told me he wasn't paying me to keep his wife happy. Lori-Anne had scurried inside so fast she nearly broke the door.

Aunt Penny sighed. "You didn't even notice, did you? She could have paraded naked across the deck and you'd have thought she was just suntanning. If you're right, if Wilkins did kill her…"

I swallowed. The mess just got a whole lot bigger. "He gets two for one."

Penny nodded. "So you better get down to the police station and tell your side of the story before he gets his all sewn up."

CHAPTER SEVEN

Outside, it was even darker than an hour ago. No moon, just a handful of stars that cast no light at all. I was all fired up when I went out Aunt Penny's door. Ready to drive straight to the police station and lay down the truth. But by the time I drove fifty feet, excuses were creeping back in. There wouldn't be any detectives there in the middle of the night. Just the routine patrol shift responsible for catching speeders and drunks.

Or worse, Constable Swan with her smirk of disbelief.

I drove slowly, practicing my story. A car came up behind me and rode my bumper, flashing its lights to get me to speed up. At the first straightaway, it pulled out and roared past, horn blasting. Then another car appeared in my rearview mirror. Bigger this time. Its lights were blinding. He sat on me for almost a mile, and I pressed harder on the gas, trying to get some speed. Farmhouses and small bungalows whizzed by without him making a move to pass.

The local detachment was still about five miles up the highway, but I remembered a gravel back road through some woods. It would take longer, but it would give me more time to practice my story without worrying about cars on my tail. The turnoff came up faster than I expected and I had to spin the wheel hard. The pickup slid sideways thirty feet across the gravel before I got it under control. The other car blew past and on down the highway.

The woods seemed even darker. No farmhouses, not even the flicker of stars to light the way. I took a deep breath. I thought of the cop station up ahead, and the steering wheel grew slick in my hands. I had the screw in my pocket, but who was going to believe it came from the deck? What if Jeff Wilkins already told the cops his version of his wife and me? Why would any woman mess with a dumb, dirt-poor handyman when she already had the richest man in the county, he'd say. The romance was all in my head, and when I figured that out, I'd killed her.

At first the headlights were far behind me. Just a quick flash as I rounded a bend. A few minutes later I saw them again. Closer. A glare of white fire in the black night.

He's going way too fast, I thought. Probably some local who's been driving this road since he was ten. Up ahead, the road opened up into a long straight stretch.

I pressed my foot on the gas. Behind me, all was dark. I relaxed my grip.

Suddenly the light from his high beams flooded my cab.

Fear shot through me. The car came up on my rear, its lights wiping out everything in my wake. On either side, pastures sloped down into a gully. At the bottom, the road curved out of sight into the trees. Still the guy stuck to me. Why the hell didn't he pass? He had plenty of room. But he sat on my bumper, his engine rumbling.

The curve in the road rushed toward me. I was going way too fast. My heart hammered. I tried to remember how sharp the curve was and what was on the other side. Trees flashed by and branches slapped my windshield. I caught a glimpse of metal railing and remembered. Too late.

The bridge!

I slammed on the brakes. Fought the wheel as I tried to aim for the narrow plank track. My truck skidded. Headlights and chrome filled my rearview mirror. I felt a violent shove from behind. Heard the bang of metal on metal. Then I was flying through the air. Branches screeched along the sides of the truck. My headlights caught bits of green and silver and rock as I cartwheeled over the edge.

It felt like a lifetime. Spinning, thumping, swooshing, before I hit the creek with a huge splash. The truck ploughed a wake through the water and shook to a stop. My engine died, my lights went out.

I hung upside down, shaking all over. Trying to make sense of the blackness. The sound of water gurgled around me. My truck was on its roof. Water was rushing in the broken windshield. Creeping up the sides. My ponytail was flopped over my ear and dragged in the water. I reached my hand over my head. I had only a couple of inches till the water would reach my head. It was pouring in fast.

I squirmed and twisted but found myself pinned by something pressing against my shoulder. My seatbelt, I realized finally. I groped around for the buckle. Pushed and pressed at the plastic until my fingers hit the right button and the belt burst open. I pitched headfirst into the cold dark water. At the last minute I twisted my head sideways to avoid crashing against the roof. Water closed over my mouth and rushed into my nostrils. I fought panic, flailed around in the tiny space to turn myself over. My feet hit the steering wheel, elbows cracked against the doors. Which way was up?

By a miracle, my head popped up above the water. Pressed against the floor of the cab. I didn't have much time. I felt for the door handle, held it and kicked the door as hard as I could. It wouldn't budge.

The water held it tight. I found the window handle and began to roll. More water poured it, almost sweeping me across the cab. I had inches of room. I remembered the car behind me, with its huge grinning lights. I took one deep, angry breath, dived down and dragged myself out the window. I got stuck halfway. Still below water, I flailed about like a fish on the line. I thought my head would burst. I kicked and shoved. The metal scraped my back as I wiggled the rest of the way out the hole. An instant later, my head came up in the silent black river.

I hung on to the truck, gasping for air and trying to calm myself. I shook all over. Where the hell was I? I peered around in the dark to see how far I was from shore. That's when I realized I wasn't alone. Headlights shone through the trees and over the water. A car was rumbling slowly across the bridge. I could see nothing but the headlights, but I heard the engine stop. A door opened and footsteps crunched on the gravel. In the spooky light, I saw a shadow walk to the side of the bridge and lean over. Peer down into the water.

Searching.

I pulled myself along the edge of my truck out of sight and ducked as low in the water as I could. Barely breathed. The lights from the car made long shadows, hiding me.

After what seemed like hours, the footsteps moved again, the door opened and the engine roared back to life. Spinning his tires on the gravel surface, the guy took off. From my hiding spot I watched as his taillights disappeared up the hill and out of sight, leaving the throaty roar of the car hanging in the air.

I had heard that lousy muffler before. At Jeff Wilkins' cottage.

CHAPTER EIGHT

"Tell me again what happened?" Constable Swan raised one eyebrow and gave me a look. At least she'd given me a blanket and turned up the heat in her cruiser before starting in on me. Didn't this woman ever sleep? Her cruiser clock said 12:02 AM. Two hours since I'd gone off the bridge. I was so tired I almost fell over in the backseat.

I'd waited a long time in the water before I decided I was safe. Then I swam ashore and hauled myself up over the rocks. I stood on the road in the dark, listening to the owls. Now what? I could just see the wheels of my pickup sticking up above the water. I almost cried. The tow and repair bills were going to wipe me out. That weasel Wilkins hadn't even paid me for the deck, and now that money was spent. If I ever saw it.

I shivered so hard my teeth clattered. Every inch of me ached and I was dizzy. I needed help. Warmth, dry clothes and a phone to call the police. I stood in the middle of the bridge, trying to remember what was nearby. I'd passed nothing but pastures and woods on my way, but then I remembered the pastures belonged to Gerry Bennett, and his dairy farm was just at the top of the hill ahead.

It was the longest hill I'd ever climbed. But Gerry's homemade plum brandy warmed me nicely while he called the police. I was well into my third glass by the time Constable Swan arrived. She whipped it out of my hand before hustling me into her car. Back down to the bridge we went, with curious Gerry trundling along behind in his tractor. In case you need help pulling it out, he said. I knew my truck needed way more help than his tractor, but I was in no shape to argue. I had to save all my wits for Constable Swan.

So I explained again about the car that ran me off the road.

"No offence, O'Toole," Swan replied, "but you're drunk as a skunk. We don't call this bridge Last Call for nothing."

She was right about that. About once a year some idiot taking a shortcut home from the Lion's Head would sail over the guard-rail into the drink. I'd even helped Bud from Bud's Garage rig a winch system that would haul the cars out of the creek without his tow truck even having to leave the road.

I concentrated hard. "I'm not drunk. I mean, I wasn't drunk. I was coming home from Wilk—" I saw her eyes narrow. "Aunt Penny's. Someone's trying to scare me off from saying what I know."

She looked up from her notebook. She was standing outside the open cruiser door, her foot resting on the running board. She leaned in to peer at me. "And what do you know?"

"That someone tampered with that deck. They changed the screws in the railing."

"And how do you know that?"

"I…" Too late, I saw I was in a box. What the hell, I decided. Better she thinks I'm a bad listener than a drunk who can't nail two pieces of wood together. "Because I found this screw in the rocks below the deck."

I wiggled my hand into my soggy pocket. The screw wasn't there. I scrounged all around, thinking it might have gotten wedged in the corner. Nothing. By now, both her eyebrows were just about disappearing under her cap.

"You went out to the scene, O'Toole? After I gave you a direct order?"

"Someone is trying to set me up," I said. "I found the wrong kind of screw at the site, but it must have fallen out in the water."

Swan waited a beat. "Set you up. And who might that be?"

I was so dead-tired I could hardly think. I had figured it was Jeff Wilkins, but now I wasn't so sure. Wilkins exchanged his vehicles the instant they got a scratch or a rattle. Rough timing and busted mufflers weren't good for business. The car that ran me off the bridge had both. Plus, it was a V8 at least twenty years older than anything Wilkins drove.

"Who, O'Toole?"

I shrugged.

Headlights shone in the distance. Both Swan and I turned to see a large flatbed truck bumping down the hill. I recognized the knocking sound of Bud's tow truck long before I could make out his name on its dusty side. It came to a rattling stop behind us. A tiny gray-haired woman climbed down. The business still carried Bud's name, but more often than not Bud was flat on his back with pain. It was his wife who took the calls. Nancy always looked like she'd been dragged out of a hen house. Hair like straw, skin like a turkey wattle and a scowl to match. When she saw my truck, though, she couldn't hide a grin.

"This is a first for you, Rick!"

I'm not much of a drinker. Even if I had the money, I don't like how stupid it makes me act. The guys tease me down at the Lion's Head when I stop in for a beer or two. But the truth is, it's those third and fourth beers that cause all the trouble. Sometimes a loosened tongue is not a good thing.

"Rick thinks he was run off the road," said Constable Swan.

Both women laughed. I glowered. "Just get my damn truck out of the creek and I'll prove it."

I was hoping the old V8 would have done some damage to my back end. I was also hoping that screw was somewhere in the bottom of my truck. Not that Swan would believe I didn't plant it.

The cop moved her cruiser so her headlights lit up the creek, and Nancy wasted no time wading out into the water and hitching the winch up to the wheels of my truck. I cringed as she slowly flipped it over in the water. But the truth was, she was good. A damn sight better than Bud, whose strength always gave out on him at the worst times. Nancy has been doing most of the garage work and all the towing in three counties since Bud was diagnosed. She looked like beaten shoe leather and had the charm of a scalded cat. But she moved those levers and gears like she was hauling a late-model Cadillac instead of a thirty-year-old pickup. Water poured through the windows as it bounced upright.

Back down to change the hitches, then up to work the gears again. By now quite a crowd had gathered, including Swan's shift supervisor, Sergeant Hurley, and a paramedic team, who seemed more interested in the damage to my truck than to me. They checked me out, bandaged a bump on my head I didn't even know I had, cleaned the cuts on my arms from the windshield and told me I should see a doctor in the morning. Fat chance of that.

All the headlights were aimed at my poor truck as it came up through the bush. Its hood and windshield were crushed, the front bumper was gone and all the lights were broken. But it was the sight of the tailgate that made me smile.

"Looks like something hit you pretty good there, Rick," Nancy said.

Swan's supervisor headed over for a closer look, and Swan hustled over to join him. Sergeant Hurley had been at the detachment for a hundred years, almost, and nothing much got by him. He was the one who took me to identify my mother, and he's had a soft spot for me ever since. Sometimes he even tries to give me fatherly advice. Or what he figures is fatherly advice. I wouldn't know, and neither would he.

Any move hurt like hell, but I wasn't missing this moment. I dragged myself out of the cruiser and limped down to the edge of the road where my truck sat dripping. Hurley was peering at the tailgate with his flashlight.

"And you think someone did this deliberately?" he asked.

"They did. An old Ford V8 with a hole in its exhaust. I heard it earlier today over at"—

65

I stopped for only a second—"Jeff Wilkins' place."

"Wilkins doesn't own a vehicle like that," Hurley said.

I squatted down an inch from the big scratch along the edge. Bits of chrome stuck to the black paint. "I bet it's at least twenty years old. All we have to do is find it. Can't be too many old souped-up V8s still on the road."

Gerry was down off his tractor, angling for a closer look. "Lots still stored under tarps in the shed, though, with owners dreaming of getting them back on the road. Nancy, I bet you and Bud see them."

Nancy nodded. "Lori-Anne Wilkins used to drive one herself, before she married Jeff."

I was surprised. "Does she still have it?"

Swan rolled her eyes. "Well, she's dead."

I felt my face grow hot in the darkness, but Nancy ignored her. "I think she gave it to her son. I told her she was nuts. Flaming death trap, that thing was."

I didn't know much about Lori-Anne's kids. I knew there was a son and a daughter. But they were a lot younger than me, so our paths didn't cross. But I remembered Lori-Anne worked late hours before she met Wilkins. And the kids ran wild in the streets of Lake Madrid long after dark. Aunt Penny always felt sorry for them. She said they'd learned to live by their wits way too young. When it got cold, they hung around the store. They always seemed to need a wash and a good meal, so Aunt Penny would give them things. She never let them steal, but she gave them apples, expired bread and chips. Said Lori-Anne needed all the help she could get. In her own way, Aunt Penny was a softie.

"Does he still live with her?" I asked. "I never saw him at the cottage."

"They're both away at college in the city," Sergeant Hurley said. I think the man knows where you're going before you do, because he added, "Jeff said he only just reached them. They won't be coming down till the funeral Friday."

"Aw, no big family hugs?" Nancy said.

Nobody seemed to think that needed an answer.

"Then I guess that means they weren't around here driving O'Toole off the road, were they," Constable Swan said. She strode around my truck. "This thing's so banged up I don't know how you can tell a damn thing."

I said nothing. Sometimes that's the best thing, with women and with cops. But it didn't stop me from thinking. It made no sense for Lori-Anne's son to be spying on me at the cottage or driving me off the road. It was his mother who'd been killed, and if he thought I had proof, surely he'd be the first person wanting the cops to have it.

But if the son did have an old, beat-up V8, Jeff Wilkins could have gotten his hands on it. I didn't know how, but I was betting Lori-Anne had spare keys around the house somewhere. Wilkins had already proved he was a resourceful guy, especially when it came to pointing the finger at some other sucker. From the sound of it, he didn't like his stepson much either.

CHAPTER NINE

The next day, I was so sore and dizzy I could hardly get out of bed. If it wasn't for Chevie nipping my feet and the hens squawking in the yard, I wouldn't have moved for a week. I sure wasn't up to tracking down a beat-up old car. I figured Jeff Wilkins would have got it back to the city somehow anyway. Maybe even got the chrome bumper fixed before the son even noticed the car was gone.

But Friday morning I was determined to get up. Lori-Anne's funeral was set for three o'clock in St. Matthew's Church, and I wanted to be there. Aunt Penny arrived out at the farm with a frozen lasagna, some day-old cinnamon buns and a big bottle of Advil. She looked none too pleased to be playing delivery boy, and bawled me out for driving around in my old rattletrap like I was in the Indy 500.

I took offence. "I was nearly killed!"

Her lips pursed. "Word is, you were drunk."

I told her about the old car, and Gerry's plum brandy. "The cops even impounded my truck. Evidence, they said. It's sitting in their lot waiting for tests."

She snorted. "Your truck is sitting outside Bud's Garage, where everybody who stops by can share the joke about your midnight swim."

I remembered Constable Swan's smirk, and a spike of anger made my head ache. The cops didn't believe me. They'd played along just to humor me. Or maybe they thought the booze and the bump on the head had gotten to me.

After Aunt Penny left, I downed two Advil and went outside. It took me a full minute to realize that with my truck gone, how was I going to get to the funeral? That whack on the head must have shaken loose a few brains. Staring at the spot of flattened weeds where I usually parked, I tried to think. Did any of my pieces of junk around here run well enough to get me all the way down the highway to the church? I still had half a dozen lawn tractors, but I wouldn't get to the funeral till Tuesday on one of them. Plus, I'd never live it down. The 4x4 in the shed had only three wheels.

That's when I remembered the dirt bike someone gave me years ago for fixing their chain saw. Aunt Penny had not been impressed with the payment, so I'd never ridden the thing. Now I limped over to the shed and dragged it out into the sunshine.

It was at least twenty years old, the seat was gone, and I was pretty sure the gears were rusted out. But it had two wheels and a 2-stroke, 250cc engine that a few shots of 10w-30 should spruce up in no time.

In fact it took three hours and a lot more than a few shots of oil, but I got it running with an hour to spare. I have one set of dress clothes—well, I call them dress clothes—so I put them on and headed off. My shirt got splattered with grease, and I sounded like a jet engine warming up as I rattled along the highway. But it looked like I was going to get there on time.

I'd expected Jeff Wilkins to put on a big show. Fancy casket, lots of pallbearers, organ, hymns and a catered spread after the burial. That way everyone would talk about how much he loved her.

But I was wrong. The bugger hadn't spent a penny more than he had to. Nothing but a short graveside service that couldn't have set him back more than the commission on a ten-year-old truck. There were only a dozen cars in the church parking lot, so only a few heads turned when I roared in off the highway. I guess not too many people mourned the death of Lori-Anne Wilkins. Aunt Penny was there, talking to Nancy the tow-truck wizard. Constable Swan was looking very classy with her peaked cap tucked under her arm and her long ponytail flowing down her back. She barely looked my way.

I rolled the dirt bike behind a bush, where I hoped no one would notice it, and started across the parking lot, scanning the cars. Jeff Wilkins' black sports coupe, looking freshly washed and waxed, took center stage among the pickups and suvs. Tucked under the branches of a huge maple that almost hid it from view was a black Ford LTD with a 351 V8 and a dented chrome bumper.

Bingo.

Aunt Penny was waving at me, but I pretended not to notice. I wanted to hang out by the back fence where I could watch everyone. I spotted Jeff Wilkins standing beside Reverend MacLeod. He had a firm grip on two teenagers, who looked like they wanted to be anywhere else. They stared at the hole in front of them. The girl was hiding behind a big hat and even bigger sunglasses. She had the same tiny frame and blond hair as her mother, but her puffy dress made her look like a hot-air balloon. Her brother had pulled his baseball cap down almost over his eyes and shoved his hands in his pockets. He looked like he wanted to kill the world, or at least Jeff Wilkins.

The minister patted Wilkins' arm and turned to face the crowd. Opening his book, he began to read. A scrap from the Bible, then a sappy prayer about living on in memory. The priest had said the same stuff at my mother's funeral. And it didn't look like it was helping any better this time. In the silence afterward, Lori-Anne's kids began to whisper to each other. I moved a little closer.

"Shut up," Wilkins hissed at them.

"Fuck you," the boy said.

"Daniel," said the minister, looking up from his prayer. "Would you like to say a few words about your mother?"

Daniel jerked like a bolt of lightning had hit. He froze, his eyes wide. Reverend MacLeod was quick off the mark and turned to Wilkins without blinking an eye. "A difficult task for a young man in such circumstances. Perhaps you'd prefer to speak, Jeff?"

And speak he did. Squeezed out the tears and the sighs, talked about how she'd gone to the angels and he hoped she hadn't suffered. Managed a dig about the careless moron who'd caused her death.

A couple of people glanced at me, including Constable Swan. I edged behind a large bush.

Reverend MacLeod thanked him and then opened his Bible for another read. The girl suddenly raised her head. "I want to say something."

Daniel and Wilkins both gave her a nervous look. Before they could object, the girl whipped off her sunglasses. Her eyes were smudged black. "I'm Bethany Tailor. Mom raised Danny and me all on her own for ten years after our dad took off. Nobody ever loved their kids more. Or worked harder to give them a good life. If this world was fair, she should have gotten a reward for that. But instead..." She stopped, her tears making black streaks down her cheeks. "She always hoped, you know? Always thought there might be better days around the corner. Better days for us. Better days for her. Mom wasn't educated or supersmart.

She liked simple things. Pretty things. All she wanted was a nice house with flowers and birds and a good life for us."

Daniel reached over to grip his sister's arm. She yanked it away. "This should have been her time for reward. She got married. She got us into college. She had time for her garden and her decorating. It wasn't... it wasn't"—she sobbed—"supposed to end like this."

Daniel leaned toward her. Whispered in her ear. She nodded, put her sunglasses back on with shaking hands and fell silent.

Beside her, Wilkins wiped away a tear. Hypocrite, I thought. A few people were wiping away tears, and pretty soon the minister cleared his throat and lifted his book.

Afterward, people walked by to shovel dirt on Lori-Anne's casket. A pine casket, I noticed. Soon I was alone in the graveyard. People headed into the church hall for refreshments, but when Wilkins put his arm around the kids to steer them inside, Bethany shook him off.

"This is all your fault!"

"Bethany, honey, it was a terrible accident."

"You bought that bird feeder. It's because of you that she's dead!"

"But I didn't know—"

"You promised you'd hang it! She said she waited days and days."

Daniel muttered something to her and tried to haul her away. "No, Danny! No! It wasn't an accident! He did this!"

Wilkins glanced in my direction and his eyes narrowed. I ducked lower, but the bush wasn't big enough.

"You never gave her a moment's happiness, you fucking control freak! It should have been you!" Bethany was wailing. "You did this on purpose, knowing—"

Daniel grabbed her shoulders and almost threw her into the old Ford.

Wilkins' jaw dropped. "Take her home, Danny," he said. "Give her one of those pills Doc Logan gave me. Just keep her the hell away from people."

The Ford peeled out of the lot, gravel spraying and muffler roaring. Wilkins watched it go, then turned to go into the church. He looked worried. He didn't turn in my direction, but I saw his eyes slide sideways toward my bush.

What the hell was all that? Wilkins with a soft side? Or playing to the audience. Me.

CHAPTER TEN

The graveyard scene bothered me all the way home. I wanted Wilkins to be guilty, but I couldn't make the Ford LTD fit into the scheme. Someone driving it had spotted me inspecting the deck, and sped away. Later they had followed me to Aunt Penny's and tried to run me off the road. I'd thought the driver was just trying to scare me off, but he did a pretty thorough job. He even got out of his car to check what happened. My truck was upside down in the creek. Normally a sign that the person inside was in trouble. But the LTD drove off and left me.

Like he wanted me dead.

Which had to mean he thought I knew what he'd done. Or had proof that could nail him.

Wilkins was a smart guy. He knew cars. It was a stretch to think that he'd gone to the city to borrow the son's car so he could sneak up on me. Now, as the dirt bike shook loose every bone in my body, I could see all the holes in my theory.

First off, Wilkins could have any car he wanted. Customers brought in trade-ins all the time. Why pick a car that stands out a mile off? Second, how did he get back home from the city after returning the car to the son? It was a hundred miles. Not a short hop. Third, he must have known the LTD was damaged and that the cops could tie it to my accident. Even I watched enough cop shows to know that.

All of this pointed one of two ways. Either Wilkins wanted to set up his stepson for the death of his mother...

Or he wasn't the one driving the Ford.

Which meant his stepson was. I hated that thought. I shoved it out of my mind, hoping it would go away or a better one would come along. Daniel was just a kid, way younger than me and with even fewer breaks in his life. Maybe Lori-Anne hadn't been the greatest mother in the world, but from what Bethany said, she'd tried. And kids forgave their mothers almost anything.

For a while, I rested my tired brain. I got home, changed my clothes, fed the animals and started tinkering with the dirt bike. Tinkering always sorts out my head. I figured I could change the 2-stroke for a 4-stroke and replace a couple of parts, like the tires and gears. Then I'd have a pretty decent set of wheels. I wasn't sure when I'd be able to pay for my truck repairs, but a guy can get a lot done towing a little trailer behind a dirt bike.

I poked around in my sheds, looking for engine parts. Despite myself, my mind wandered back to the LTD. Why would Wilkins set up his stepson? From the sound of it, there was no love lost between them. But both kids would be out of his life before the grass was green on Lori-Anne's grave. Would they be making off with some of his money? That would sure piss him off. But I couldn't see how, since he was the one still alive.

Besides, how did Wilkins know I'd be going over to inspect the deck? How would he know ahead of time so he could get Daniel's car? I didn't like the guy. I thought he was a weasel who treated his wife like crap and was ready to let me take the blame for her death. But I didn't think he was psychic. This theory didn't make sense.

Which brought me back to Daniel. I wandered out into my back field to look at the lawn tractors. A couple of them had 4-stroke engines that might work on my dirt bike. Horsepower wasn't an issue. Some of these buggers weighed a ton.

The kids weren't in town, that's the thing. They were away at college. How could Daniel have sneaked back to tamper with the deck? And more importantly, why? From what I'd heard, they both loved their mother and wanted the best for her. The best was obviously not Jeff Wilkins. But he was rich and better than nothing.

Unless...

I remembered the thought I had earlier. *He was the one still alive.* My heart raced. Suddenly a whole new bunch of possibilities opened up. If Wilkins was dead, Lori-Anne would inherit his fortune. She would be free of his tight-ass, controlling ways. She wouldn't have to sit at home watching daytime TV and begging to use one of his cars. Her kids could drive to college in something better than a flaming death trap. They would have money for clothes, trips and partying. They would see their mother finally getting the happiness she deserved.

What if the deck accident had been meant for him and not her?

I hardly breathed so I wouldn't disturb my brain. Did that make sense? How could Lori-Anne have set it up? If she'd known the deck was dangerous, surely she'd never have leaned on it, unless she was so drunk she forgot the danger. That seemed to take her off the suspects list.

But her son? I remembered that look of pure hatred on his face as he stood at Wilkins' side. But even if he sneaked back from school and replaced the screws, he was taking a terrible risk. How could he be sure Wilkins would lean on it and not his mother? Maybe he thought the tiny woman wouldn't break the rail, but hefty, beer-swilling Wilkins would?

I sat down on the tractor with a thud. Had Daniel tried to set it up? Had their mother told them about the feeder, and how Wilkins was going to hang it for her? Had he seen his chance for a perfect crime?

Almost perfect. Except for two small problems. His mother.

And me.

CHAPTER ELEVEN

The phone was ringing when I rounded the barn. I got about two phone calls a week, if you didn't count Aunt Penny or some scammer from the city. A phone call meant money, so I ran to answer it. My sore muscles weren't happy, but I figured they'd get over it.

There was no one there. Empty air. Usually this means one of those computers from the city, dialing up numbers by chance. But this sounded different. Not an annoying hum but a rumble.

And I thought I could hear breathing. Soft, like they were holding it in. Listening.

Then Chevie went racing down the lane, barking her head off. I peered out the front window. There was nothing there, but in the distance down by the main road a cloud of dust hung in the air. On the phone, I heard the roar of a car, accelerating away. Followed by nothing.

I hung up, my heart beating. I stared out the window. Nothing but the late afternoon sun and the crickets. I was imagining things. I was freaked out by the accident and my mind was playing tricks. Who would be calling? Who would be cruising past my house? Daniel? Why? To scare me, or to check out my home? He was just a kid. This seemed way more sinister than anything he could do. I still hated the idea that he tampered with the deck.

Maybe I was missing something. Wilkins knew much more about decks than Daniel did, and had a much better chance to switch the screws. He knew his wife was impatient about the feeder. He'd been stalling so long, it was almost like he drove her to it.

I wished I could walk away. If Daniel was guilty, I wasn't sure I wanted him caught. The kids had had a rough start. I knew what that could do to a kid. And he'd already been punished way more than any court would do. Killing his own mother was a nightmare he'd never forget.

If Wilkins was guilty, I didn't know how I could prove it. Nobody believed me. The screw was at the bottom of the creek, and all the other signs, like the old Ford, pointed away from him. The bastard had already slapped a lawsuit on me to make sure the fingers didn't point to him.

It was that thought that really got me going. I wasn't going to let Wilkins sue me for every last blade of grass on my farm. I wasn't going to let the whole county think I'd killed a woman because I couldn't design a deck to save my life. Not to mention I'd driven my truck into Silver Creek in a drunken stupor.

I couldn't walk away. I had to prove, once and for all, who had killed Lori-Anne Wilkins.

The best way would be a confession. I was betting tempers were pretty raw at the Wilkins' place by now, and nobody would be holding back. If I could get close enough to hear, I'd probably learn all I needed to. I pictured the long laneway up to the cottage. Most of it was shielded by bush, so no one would see my approach, and when I got close enough, I could sneak along the foundation to an open window.

I went outside, full of purpose, and caught sight of my dirt bike in the side yard. Crap. No one would see my approach, but they'd sure as hell hear it. I'd have to walk the last half mile in, or they'd all be waiting on the front porch for me. And even if I got there unnoticed, even if I got my confession, who was going to believe me? So far, it was Wilkins three, me zip. I needed proof. I needed a recording.

I've never really liked technology. It takes you too far away from nature. Blame it on my Mom, who spent more time with Elvis and *Dynasty* reruns that she ever did with real life. I like to hear the sounds of the birds and even the goat chomping my daisies more than the sound of the latest rock band. I like to sit on my front porch watching the sunsets and the hay turning golden in the fall more than I like to sit in a dark, stuffy room. Television is about ridiculously pretty people making morons of themselves. I own a TV and a phone, like I said, but I never bothered with radios or CD players or computers. Don't get me started on computers.

Still, there are times a tape recorder would come in handy. Like now. I wondered if Aunt Penny had one I could borrow, but then she'd want to know why and she'd give me that look. Not worth it.

I started wandering around my sheds, looking for possibilities. That's another reason I don't like technology. It's always changing, and old parts don't fit new things. You can't just stick things together and experiment. You need a microscope to see what you're doing, and a shot of 10w-30 is no help at all. Why can't something that worked fine thirty years ago still work fine today?

That's when it hit me. I did have something. My mother hoarded everything. You never knew when you might need it, she said. And if you didn't, you could always sell it at a yard sale. When I was a baby, she had this little baby monitor. It had a transmitter that went in my room and a receiver in her room. It transmitted every sound

I made—every cry and burp—down to the room where she was watching TV. Sometimes she carried it out to the barn or vegetable garden. They had a pretty good range, those little things. Once I'd used it to warn me when a cat was going into labor in the back barn a hundred yards from the house. If I planted one inside the Wilkins' house and hid down the lane, I should be able to hear everything.

I knew exactly where the baby monitor was. Aunt Penny thinks my place is just a jumble, but it's not. It took me less than thirty seconds to reach the shed, get up on the stool and pull it down from the top shelf. I had to replace the batteries, but then it worked as well as the day the kittens were born. But I still had a problem. I needed a way to record what I heard.

Mom to the rescue again. This time the old tape recorder she'd bought at a yard sale to tape Elvis off the radio. I'd never used it, but I remembered her using it well enough. Sitting on the porch with that dreamy look in her eyes. Swaying to the music from this black box. She'd turn the radio up really loud and then press the Record button on the tape machine. That should work. That cat's yowling had sounded really loud on the baby monitor.

I popped the lid and saw there was still some tape in the cassette. I dusted it off, put in new batteries and gave the thing a quick test. By some miracle, it still worked. Maybe for once, the old guy upstairs had decided to humor me.

I stuffed all the electronics into a backpack and revved up the dirt bike. The sun was getting low in the sky, making it hard to see. But that meant the shadows would be deep and it would be easier to hide. I roared along the highway, through the village and past the church. The parking lot was empty now, the wake over.

About half a mile up Wilkins' road I killed the engine, hid the bike in the brush and walked up the gravel lane. I stuck to the edge so I could dive out of sight if I had to. I felt jumpy as a cat. My heart thumped, and sweat soaked my shirt under the pack.

The parking area in front of the cottage was empty. No sign of the old Ford or Wilkins' car. The cottage sat in the shadows, spooky and still. I crouched down and ran up to the front window. Nearly had a heart attack when the security lights flooded the scene. I dove for cover. Nothing happened. I crept back and pressed my ear to the wall. Nothing. No voices. No sounds of music or TV. I peered inside but everything was dark. I ducked and ran along to the next window. That room was dark too. I circled the house, checking out the kitchen, the bedrooms and all three bathrooms. No one was home.

Perfect luck. I worked one of the windows until it slid open. I climbed inside, hauling my backpack with me. A loud beeping almost sent me through the roof. I was so spooked I'd forgotten the alarm! Lucky for me, Wilkins had given me the code so I could come and go. Hands shaking, I punched it in, and the clamor stopped.

I stood in the living room, straining to hear. Nothing. In the stillness I pictured the dead woman standing in the middle of the room, giving me that little wave.

The silence was eerie. I wondered where they all were. It didn't seem like family outings were high on their list. I stuck the baby transmitter into a palm tree in the corner of the living room. Lori-Anne's palm tree. She'd said she was hoping it would grow tall and make her feel like she was on a tropical island.

I shivered, feeling her ghost again. As fast as I could, I crawled back out the window and hightailed it down the lane. I expected to see headlights or hear the purr of Wilkins' car any moment. There was nothing. The crickets cheeped, the frogs croaked and, far off, a coyote yipped. I found my bike and crawled in beside it, careful to pull the bushes back in front of us.

Then I dug the baby monitor and tape recorder out of the backpack and settled down to wait.

CHAPTER TWELVE

Darkness fell. I cursed my stupidity. I'd forgotten a jacket. I'd forgotten to eat supper or put on bug spray. Even in September, the little buggers were out in force. I curled my arms around myself and tried to be small while I waited.

The sound of a broken muffler woke me with a start. I peered at my watch: 9:05. The Ford rumbled by me. It was too dark to see inside, but I sat up at attention. I listened as the car growled to a stop and car doors slammed. Distant voices drifted toward me. One girl, one boy.

Loud and angry. Good. I pressed the Record button and waited to see if my contraption would work.

For a minute, nothing. Then vague sounds crackled through the receiver. A thud, the clink of bottles. Then a voice, so loud I jumped out of my skin.

"I can't believe there was nothing! Not a fucking penny!" Bethany said.

"Why should there be? Mom didn't have a penny of her own. He made sure of that."

"He made sure of a whole lot of things." A loud *thump*. "Goddamn bastard."

Bethany must have been right beside the palm tree, because her voice just about broke my ear drum. But Daniel had gone farther away. The kitchen, maybe? He muttered something I couldn't hear.

"Somebody had to say it," Bethany replied. "It was true. This was all his fault."

"Bethany, I'm sick of this!" Daniel had come back into the room, shouting. "Can't you see what's right in front of your eyes? This isn't his fault! He's a moron, he's a tightwad, he's an asshole, but he didn't kill Mom. Face it!"

"But if he'd hung that bird feeder like he promised. If he hadn't been so lazy that she finally got fed up. This would never have happened!"

More thumps. "So he was lazy! Jesus Christ, it wasn't him that fucked up. Face that, at least."

Bethany started to wail. "Don't turn on me, Danny. I haven't slept a wink since it happened. *I didn't know!* She said he was going to hang it as soon as the deck was finished. There wasn't much time."

"Then you should have warned her!"

"Warn her how, Danny? Say, 'Oh, by the way, Mom, I'm planning to unscrew the railing so your bastard husband falls off the cliff, so don't lean on it?' You know she wanted him dead, Danny. How many times did she talk about how great it would be?"

My heart was racing, my hands were slick with sweat. I could hardly breathe through my horror. *Bethany!* I watched the tape recorder, making sure the red light was on and the spools turning.

"Yeah, but that was just dreaming," Daniel said. "That's all Mom ever did. She'd live her whole life dreaming."

"And I was sick of it!" Bethany shouted, so loud I jumped a foot. "When I heard about the bird feeder, I thought, This is our chance!"

"Some chance! Mom's dead, and for what? Less than nothing! Jesus. At least before, the bastard was paying our college fees to keep us out of his hair."

"He still might. He said he would."

Daniel snorted. "Get real, Bethany. He'll forget us tomorrow. The guy's got at least twenty years. He's going to snag some other stupid woman with stars in her eyes, and then we'll lose it all." A chair scraped and Daniel's voice began to fade. "But that's not our biggest problem right now."

"What?"

Silence. The clink of glasses. "What do you think?"

"The handyman?"

"Yeah." Daniel said something else, but I couldn't hear.

"What do we do?" Bethany asked.

I turned up the receiver as loud as I could, but Daniel's voice was still a mumble. Everything echoed. I started walking up the road, balancing the receiver on top of the recorder.

"You should never have tried to run him off the road," Daniel was saying. "Nobody would have listened to him."

"I tried to fix it, but he has that damn dog. I couldn't get close enough," Bethany said.

I nearly dropped the recorder. So that car at my farmhouse had been her!

"Wait!" Daniel's voice was sharp.

"I'll think of something else, Danny. He's got propane tanks in his yard, and lots of junk that could blow up—"

"Shut up! I hear something!"

I froze. I heard footsteps, the front door opening.

"Fuck, there's somebody out there," Daniel said. His real voice, not the receiver. I was that close. I turned and pelted down the lane. The receiver fell to the ground, but I hung on to the recorder like my life depended on it. Maybe it did.

I heard footsteps behind me. I had to get to my bike. I had to get it started and get the hell out of there, all with only a fifteen-second head start. There was no way. I veered off into the bushes. Raspberry canes ripped my skin as I ploughed through them. A few yards in, I stopped and crouched down. My heart hammered so loud I was sure they could hear it in the next county. I tried not to breathe.

Daniel and Bethany came running down the lane, cursing and slipping. Suddenly the footsteps stopped.

"What's that?" Bethany's voice.

I strained my ears but heard nothing but breathing. Then "What the fuck?"

"What is it?" Bethany whispered.

"It's…" Daniel's voice was puzzled. "I don't know. Goddamn it, it's some kind of fucking bug!"

"A bug!" Bethany shrieked. "You mean, someone—?"

"Sh-h!!" Daniel's voice dropped to a whisper. I ducked my head and held my breath. Slowly they began to walk again. Toward me. I could hardly see them in the weak light of the stars, but I could hear their footsteps. Coming along the edge of the road like they were looking in the bushes.

"We need a flashlight," Daniel said. Practical guy, this Daniel. Bethany was the one with the emotion. "You keep an eye while I get one." He turned to head back.

"Don't leave me here!"

"Oh, for fuck's sake! It's your fault we're in this mess. Your fault, Bethany! Own it, for once."

I heard her scurrying after him. He seemed to give up the fight, and they both disappeared into the house.

I scrambled back out of the bushes. I figured I had at most a minute before they found a flashlight and came back. I ran down the rest of the lane, not caring how much noise I made. Found my bike, dragged it out onto the road and shoved the recorder into the backpack. I started to run, pushing the dirt bike and hoping it would catch. Finally, I heard the weak, sputtering sound. Louder, more regular. Then the engine flared to life. Noisy as hell. I heard shouts behind me, heard the sounds of car doors slamming before it was all drowned out by the sound of a jet plane and the wind in my ears.

CHAPTER THIRTEEN

I'd driven this road lots of times in the past month, so I knew every turn and pothole. The dirt bike was nimble. Much nimbler than a huge old Ford with no shocks. But the Ford had power to spare on the straight stretches, and just when I thought I'd lost them, they roared back into the game. I heard the thunder of the broken muffler as they floored it. I opened up the bike's throttle and hung on to the handlebars, praying like hell the bald tires would hold.

I kept my lead on the twisty back roads, but the highway was coming up ahead.

It had smooth pavement and long straight parts. My thoughts raced. What other choices did I have? The bike could handle off-road, but the tires might not. If I got stuck or flipped it, I'd be a sitting duck. I didn't want to think about what they might do. They were kids who'd gotten in over their heads, but that made them even more dangerous. *Blowing up my propane tanks?*

A few houses flashed by, with lights glowing in windows. I thought of running inside, but there might be children. Old people. I couldn't put more people in danger. I was amazed how clearly I figured that out through my panic. I needed the police. The cop station was a good five miles away once I reached the main highway. Five miles was way too far if I wanted to stay alive. Think! Think!

Then I remembered. Up ahead there was an old logging road that led to the edge of Silver Creek. Once there had been a log bridge across the creek for people to walk across. On the other side, the logging road continued and met up with the highway about a mile from the station. As a kid, I used to play on the road with my bike, replacing the logs as they rotted. But that was a long time ago. Could I get through? Would it kill my engine?

Behind me, the Ford's headlights grew huge.

If not for those headlights, I would have missed the turnoff. It was overgrown with weeds and brush. I leaned hard, put my foot down and swerved onto the track. Branches whipped my face and stung my eyes. I jolted and slid, fighting to hang on. I heard the Ford shoot past the turn, slide to a stop and back up. A moment later, headlights flooded the track. Damn, they were going to try it!

The middle of the track was overgrown with tall weeds that hit my legs as I raced past. Stones and potholes came at me out of the dark. I dodged, stomped the brake, twisted the gas and worked my way deep into the woods. Up ahead, the creek glinted in my weak headlight. I approached it full speed. If I was going to get across, I had to have momentum. I had to fly. Up close, I panicked. There were no logs!

Too late! I couldn't stop.

I bent over the handlebars, gritted my teeth and pulled up at the last second. For a few yards, the bike sailed through the air before hitting the surface. Water swooshed around me. The bike slithered. Coughed. Mud and weeds closed in, and the bike stopped.

Behind me, I heard the rumbling Ford. I jumped off the bike. Sank into water to my knees. I tugged, pushed, shoved, dragged.

Slowly the bike came out of the mud. More shoving and I was up on the other bank, pushing the bike along the track to shake loose the mud. The engine caught again. I shouted aloud, not caring if they heard me. My hands shook with the terror of my near escape. Take that, you bastards!

Jumping aboard, I headed to the highway. Almost there now. Suddenly, amazingly, headlights lit the woods behind me. They had made it across!

How the hell?

That old Ford had more rust holes than floorboards. It must have hit the water fast enough to plane across. It was a race now. I still had the advantage in the woods, but that last mile on the highway would be a killer. I pushed the bike as fast as I dared, bending low to avoid being swept off by branches.

In minutes, I bounced up the ditch and onto the highway. It shone black and straight ahead of me, its broken white line snaking down the middle. The police station was in the middle of nowhere so it could serve the whole county. During the day, it was a busy road, but at night there was usually nothing but transport trucks. Even one of those would be welcome, but tonight there was nothing.

I maxed the gas and aimed the bike. The Ford did the same. I didn't dare look back to see how close they were, but I knew they were gaining. What would they do? Run me off the road again? I gulped. This time I wouldn't stand a chance.

Something metal flashed in my headlights as I sped by a turnoff. A moment later, new lights lit the road from behind. Red and blue. A siren screamed. I eased up and turned to look just as a police car pulled alongside me. Trembling, I steered the bike onto the shoulder and wobbled to a stop. The Ford shot past and around the bend ahead. As I turned off the engine, the cop car pulled in front of me, and Constable Swan climbed out.

I was never so happy to see anyone in my life.

CHAPTER FOURTEEN

Sergeant Hurley put out an all-call. He brought in all the off-duty cops and neighboring detachments to help in the search. The little detachment was full of cops lounging against tables, drinking coffee and trading stories about Wilkins, Lori-Anne and her messed-up children. They acted like they'd seen trouble coming a mile off.

"She knew exactly what she was getting when she married Wilkins," Parker said. Parker was all heart. "His name, his status—"

"And a jealous streak a mile wide," said a female cop. "He kept her like a bird in a cage."

"Aw, come on," the guy said. "That big fancy cottage is hardly a cage. Some women don't know when they're well-off."

"Jeez, Parker, you can't blame her for what her kids did," the woman said.

"They were kids," Parker said. "Bethany's what—eighteen? All her life Lori-Anne's fed her nothing but sob stories about her hard life. Not that she ever tried to get ahead on her own. One man after another."

The rest of them all looked at him, and I wondered if he'd been one of those men himself. I didn't like listening to them picking people apart like this. People screw up. They want things and they don't know how to get them. I was no better. I knew everyone laughed at me behind my back because I collected junk everyone else thought was worthless. I saw it differently. And it was my life after all.

I was sitting in the big chair behind the desk, wrapped in a blanket, while a paramedic put ointment on all my scratches and bites. No one was paying much attention to me. But in the interview room behind, I could hear the recording I had made. Swan and Hurley were in there, listening to it. They'd laughed when I first brought the recorder out of my backpack. It was big and clunky, and I had to show them how it worked. Then they stopped laughing.

The phone rang on the desk, and one of the cops picked it up. He listened a moment, then gave a thumbs-up. "Hold on, I'll ask the Sergeant what he wants done with them."

He put the phone down and spoke as he headed toward the back room. "They caught the kids fixing a flat just the other side of Silver Falls. Couldn't get a peep out of them. They just sat on the curb and cried. Silver Falls Detachment is bringing them back up here."

"Well, we've got all the admission we need on tape, thanks to Rick here."

They all laughed. Hurley came to the phone, and I got up to give him space. Picturing the kids sitting on the curb, I felt bad. I knew they'd tried to kill me, but I couldn't help thinking, sometimes people just find themselves in a dark place they never planned on.

I wandered toward the back room. Constable Swan looked up. She looked tired, like she'd had one shift too many, but she smiled at me. A wide, friendly smile, nothing like her usual smirk. It surprised me, and I found myself smiling back. Feeling better.

"This is quite the invention, O'Toole. Not the latest technology, but it did the trick."

She looked down at her boots, big and clumsy on her small frame. "I'm glad you came out of this all right."

I didn't say a word. A rush of blood tied my tongue in knots. But I didn't feel tired and sore anymore, and I had a funny feeling in my gut. Maybe this new technology stuff was worth another look after all. There might even be some money in it.

BARBARA FRADKIN is a child psychologist with a fascination for how we turn bad. She is best known for her gritty detective series featuring Ottawa Police Inspector Michael Green. She won Arthur Ellis Best Novel Awards for both *Fifth Son* (2005) and *Honour Among Men* (2007).

Titles in the Series

RAPID READS